Shadows on the Moon

A Lizard and Bungle Adventure

Jolyon Byerley

Illustrations by Katie Shears

CARIBBEAN

2

In the tall green islands of the West Indies, the early mornings sparkle like the jewels on the Queen of England's crown. From deep in the rain forests, lazy spirals of charcoal smoke curl up through the cool air to tickle the tummies of the clouds. This was the favourite time of day for the young Lizard who lived in a tropical garden at the foot of the mountain.

Being an adventurous sort of fellow, he often went for long walks as the sun came climbing over the high mountains. He would nuzzle his inquisitive nose into the scarlet hibiscus blossoms until the delicious golden pollen made him sneeze. Tiny hummingbirds thought this was very funny. They were hardly bigger than butterflies. Their laughter made a noise like little bells as they flew around his head. Lizard loved this tinkling sound and happily waved his incredibly long tail as he

        slithered

          up

              the mountain path.

He was really very fond of his tail and, as he grew older,
he found that he possessed a very special tail indeed.
He could make it into an 'S' shape or a circle, and
even scratch the back of his head with it.
Sometimes other island animals would
sit and watch him make shadow
pictures on a wall by the light
of the moon.

4

This particular morning he was on his way to meet his friend, the Bungle, a charming bird, who usually sat on a tree stump and thought about flying. You see, the Bungle had never actually found out how to fly. He had tried running and flapping. He had tried jumping and flapping. Once he had even been towed into the air by a friendly Pelican. But each time he had ended his flights upside down on the ground.

So now the Bungle Bird spent most of his days just sitting and thinking.

'Hello, Bungle,' cried Lizard as the two friends met.
'Let's climb up the mountain today.'
So off they went.

As they climbed, they loved to sing with gusto. Sometimes they would sing all sixty-five choruses of the Bungle Boogie with gallons of gusto and you would be amazed how quickly the hours slipped by.

'The Bungle Boogie
Boo-oo-oo!'

Soon the whole island stretched out beneath them, the green fields of sugar cane giving way to a mysterious blue carpet which stretched to the end of the world. The Bungle, who was seldom completely right, said the carpet was called 'The Big Blue Sea'. Lizard vaguely wondered if 'The Big Blue Sea' was good to eat. He was always a little hungry.

Just then, a shadow passed over them and Lizard looked up into the brilliant sky. A great shining object was flashing overhead, leaving a strange white wake behind it.

The Bungle, like his parents and grandparents before him, could not look up without falling over backwards. He lay on the ground and began to tremble.

'That,' he said shakily, 'is most definitely a Dragon.'

Lizard was not so sure. His mother had told him about wondrous flying machines that could take you to 'other places' if you were not careful. She was an educated creature, who had once been to Kalamazoo.

Suddenly, the object in the sky came streaking down
towards the top of the mountain. There was a loud bang
and then silence.

Lizard looked worried.

'Whatever that was, I think it's in trouble!' he said to the
Bungle. 'Perhaps we should hurry and see if we can help.'

They began to trot up
the steep mountainside.

But small animals seldom travel great distances and soon
the two friends became very hot and tired. So they were rather
pleased to find their path blocked by a rushing mountain
stream.

'Well, that's it, then,' said the Bungle, relieved. 'Now we
can go home for some tea and chocolate cake.'

But Lizard remembered the exploits of his great uncle, General Iguana. He was an explorer who had achieved heroic deeds, like discovering the poles.

So, after a refreshing drink from the rushing stream, he slowly backed into the tumbling water and carefully stretched out his long tail until the very end nearly reached the other side.

'Now, quickly, Bungle!' he cried. 'Hold out your wings to balance yourself and walk across my tail.'

His unsteady friend did as he was told. With eyes as big as mushrooms, he wobbled across until he reached the end of Lizard's tail.

'What shall I do now?' he called, looking round, very worried.

Lizard could only just support the Bungle Bird's weight. He became a little desperate.

'Jump Bungle! Jump the rest of the way.'

And, do you know, something rather wonderful happened then!
The Bungle, gathering all his courage, leapt into the air and began
flapping his little wings harder than ever before.

Perhaps it was just a lucky gust of wind,
but

the Bungle

began

to fly!

Because his toes were clamped
tightly around his friend's tail,
Lizard was also pulled into the air
and they both landed in a heap
on the other bank.

'Oh, my goodness gracious me!' gasped the
astounded bird. 'Did that really, really happen?'
'Bungle, I'm proud of you,' said Lizard. He was
shaking with excitement because it was the first time he had
flown, too.

At that moment, a Dreaded Hairy Globule stepped out of his hole. Gallantly doffing his top hat, he held out his hand.

'May I introduce myself?' he said. 'I am D. H. Globule, Esq., Gentleman retired. And you must be the famous explorers, Lizard and the Bungle. May I tempt you to a nice cup of tea?'

They all crowded into the Globule's hole and Lizard explained why they were climbing up the mountain. D. H. Globule was immediately intrigued.

Pray allow me to be your companion upon this noble adventure,' he said.

So, after tea and a slice of splendid coconut pie, they began once more on the long climb to the top, this time singing 'The Marching Song of The Globules' (with, of course, gallons more gusto).

'Nor-ma-lly, after tea
the dreaded Globs go marching!
Red boots on our feet
in case we should meet
a King and a Queen out walking.
　　Sing Glob (loud)
　　Sing Glob (louder)
　　SING GLOB (VERY LOUD)'

Music composed and arranged
by the Beetle.

Now, in the Caribbean, the big orange sun goes to bed quite early. The moon and the stars are so bright that many animals carry on chatting long into the night. You may sometimes find Bananaquits and Pearly Eyed Thrashers playing games like Blog (a sort of hopscotch) well after supper. The wild goats become quite frisky in the moonlight, chasing each other through the shadows on their hind legs. More like a herd of Kangas, really.

The most wide awake of all are the little Tree Frogs, who are no bigger than a button. They sit on a comfortable leaf and sing songs to each other all through the velvet night.

'Beep, beep, beep,' goes one.

'Churrp, churrp, churrp,' answers another.

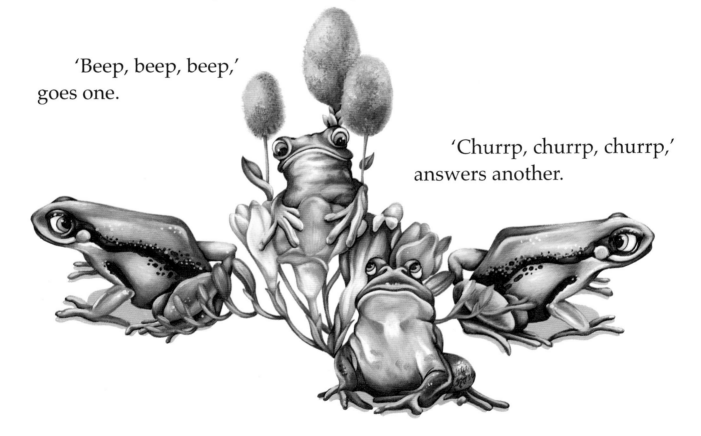

So Lizard and his friends were really not worried about continuing their journey in the dark. Until, that is, they took the wrong path. Now, the trees of a tropical forest stand close together and their leaves cover the earth like a great green umbrella. No matter how bright the moon and stars, the night was suddenly very dark indeed. From every nook and cranny, the eyes of a hundred different night creatures glowed like little candles on a Birthday cake. 'I say, you chaps,' said the Dreaded Hairy Globule. 'Perhaps we should … er … sing a little louder, and … er … I think we should er … all hold hands.'

In the trees above them,
the Tree Rat was chatting to his second cousin,
the Fruit Bat.

'Jolly dark tonight, Batty,' said the Rat. Batty, who
could see better at night than in the daytime, was about to
respond when, from down on the ground beneath them,
came a most untuneful sound. The cousins both peered
down to see what on earth it could be.

Lizard, the Bungle and D. H. Globule, singing loudly,
came into sight below.

Just then a big Land Crab scuttled across the path of Lizard and his friends, bringing them and their singing to an abrupt halt.

'Nor-ma-lly, after tea
the dreaded Globs go marching!
Red boots on our feet
in case we should meet…'

'Caramba, I like that song,' said the big Land Crab, who was known in entertainment circles as Crab Far See. 'Do you know any Calypso, Man?'

Well it so happened that the Dreaded Hairy Globule had a step-brother called Hairy Belafonte Globule. From him, D. H. Globule had learned many island songs. So, accompanying himself with a dried pod from a flamboyant tree (called a Shak Shak), D. H. Globule, Gentleman, Rtd., began singing an old calypso. The Crab, listening intently, immediately picked up the rhythm. Jumping onto the back of a passing Tortoise, he began to dance. Snapping his large claws like a Flamenco dancer, he whirled and twirled in the darkness. Sometimes he moved so quickly that only his glowing eyes could be seen.

Even Batty and Ratty came down from their tree and joined in the singing and dancing.

'Dayo, dayo,' they all chorused.

When it was over, everybody applauded each other.

'Caramba, that will be a hit at the Crab Hole Club,' said the breathless dancing Crab. 'Perhaps you could come and see me dance tonight?'

Lizard, who had been dancing with his own tail, suddenly remembered what they were really supposed to be doing.

'I am terribly sorry, Mr Far See, but we are on our way to help somebody who may be in trouble at the top of the mountain,' he explained.

Everyone was quiet for a moment.

'In that case,' said the Crab, 'I, the famous Crab Far See, will accompany you.'

'And so will we,' said Batty and Ratty.

And off they all went.

In the cool of the night, they made good progress. By the time the morning sky was becoming as pink as a Bungle Bird's blush and all the birds in the forest were waking up, the friends had reached the very top of the mountain. They had been shown a short cut by a Toad in a Boy Scout hat, who also decided to join in the expedition.

'Be prepared, be prepared,' was all the Toad seemed to say.

But nothing could have prepared them for the extraordinary sight which came into view as the sun came over the surrounding hills.

Lying on its side on the mountain's very top was a great Space Ship. Its masts and sails were like those of an old Spanish Treasure Galleon. A strange humming sound came from somewhere inside, but the sails lay still and nothing stirred. On the bow of the ship was the figurehead of a large Duck.

Written on the side in green letters was the name:

S.S. PEEKING DUCK

They all stood around and gaped. Suddenly, from behind the hull of the Space Ship, the figure of a wild-eyed Duck in a silver space suit appeared.

'Aha,' said the Duck in a loud quacking voice, 'I am zee Capitaine à l'Orange, Space Duck Extraordinaire and Commander of the Clouds.' He paused for effect.

Nobody said a word.

'Are you all deaf?' quacked the Space Duck. 'It is I, Commander of the Clouds who has run aground … er … landed amongst you lesser creatures.'

He looked anxiously up at the open door of the great Space Ship which was well beyond his reach.

'And, unless I can somehow get back inside my wonderful vessel very quickly, it is programmed to cast off without me.' A large tear began to roll down his shiny yellow beak.

The friends shifted uncomfortably, No-one knew what to say or do. Who was this strange Duck and where had this peculiar Space Ship come from?

Then a much smaller Duck, also dressed in a natty little silver suit, strutted out from behind Capitaine à l'Orange, who immediately straightened up and saluted.

'May I present Prince Whistling Tree Duck, heir to the throne of Planet Pluto,' quacked the Commander of the Clouds. 'We have been trying to call Earth on Pluto Harbour Radio for years. Now we have voyaged gallons of miles through space so that the Prince may eat a Ba-na-na-na-na.'

'Peep, peep, Ba-na-na-na-na,' peeped the Prince, flapping his little fluffy wings in excitement.

D. H. Globule, Esq., looked deeply concerned. 'Oh, my dear chap,' he exclaimed, 'That, at least, is no problem.' And, reaching up above his head, he plucked a delicious golden banana from an overhanging stalk.

At first the little Prince from Planet Pluto tried to gobble the fruit without peeling back the skin. Lizard and his friends quickly lost their shyness and showed him what to do. Down went that banana in no time at all. Everyone beamed with gallons of pleasure, except for Capitaine à l'Orange.

'Thank you for the Ba-na-na-na-na, my new comrades...but...if we are not inside our Space Ship in just a few minutes we will both be left behind...and the Prince will never see his Palace, his Dad, and Planet Pluto again.'

Lizard looked thoughtful. 'Bungle, I have an idea,' he said. Quickly, he explained his plan. 'Back at the rushing river, you managed to fly just a little. If you could actually fly up to the Space Ship's open door, carrying the end of my tail, the two Space Ducks could scramble up and climb aboard – just in the nick of time!'

At first the Bungle looked doubtful and worried. But, with his friends shouting, 'Bung-gel, Bung-gel, Bung-gel,' the timid Bungle Bird they knew became a hero. His chest feathers were puffed out, his beak was lifted to the clouds and his eyes became steely blue.

'Yes,' he said in a deeper than usual voice, 'I will do it!'

The friends formed a circle around Lizard, the Bungle and the two Space Ducks.

'Stand back, stand back, give them room,' commanded D. H. Globule importantly.

Lizard flexed his tail and the Bungle stood on tiptoe and stretched his wings. It was time for the great test.

'Take hold of the very end of my tail, Bungle,' said Lizard in a very determined voice. Everyone held their breath. You could have heard a Hummingbird whisper.

'Now,' said Lizard. 'If you're ready, Bungle my old friend …

GO,

GO,

GO!'

And, as the friends erupted into excited stomping, clapping and shouting, the Bungle began to flap his wings, slowly at first, then faster and even faster. Dust flew, feathers blew and some Butterflies thought the Hurricane Season had arrived. And the Bungle who had never actually flown UP before, was climbing steadily into the air. With him went the end of Lizard's tail.

But, horrors! Lizard's tail was just not long enough to reach the open door.

'Caramba!' howled Crab Far See. 'Jump on my back quickly!'

From the extra height of the Crab's back, Lizard's tail only barely reached the door. But the Bungle had made it!

'Up, up, up you go,' everyone shrieked at the Space Ducks. And they all helped with heaving and shoving from below.

Capitaine à l'Orange and his young Prince stepped triumphantly aboard the great Space Ship. At that very moment, a loud creaking noise came from the hull and the huge sails filled with wind.

The Bungle, much to his surprise, glided smoothly and gracefully back down to his cheering friends and the two Space Ducks barely had time to wave farewell before the door of the PEEKING DUCK clanged shut.

Then, right before their eyes, the great Space Ship took off, as silently as the flight of a Bat, to begin its long journey back to Pluto.

In little more than a blink of Ratty's eyes, it had disappeared.

The friends stood around and looked at each other.

'Well, well, well!' said D. H. Globule. 'What a day!'

Lizard was very tired and his tail was aching terribly. But he waved to his friends to follow him and started to lead the way down the long path home.

It was then that the ghastly discovery was made. The animals following behind were shocked!

'Lizard's beautiful and famous tail has gone!'

'Simply not there!'

'Disappeared!'

When he heard the cries of despair, Lizard looked round. Only an ugly stump remained in place of his beautiful tail.

He was too surprised to be upset. Just a few moments before, he had thought his tail was aching. But now, there it was – gone!

'My dear, dear friend,' said the Globule, 'What absolutely rotten luck! It must have become trapped when the door of the Space Ship closed. No-one noticed in the excitement. Now your tail is on its way with the Prince to Planet Pluto.'

Lizard was sad, but more worried about the things his mother might say when he returned home without his tail.

The Bungle was deep in thought and had not said a word since his gallant flight and glide back to earth. But he felt stronger and somehow very grown up. He was even able to look up at the sky without falling over backwards.

It was then that he saw the little silver umbrella, floating down towards them.

'I'll get it,' he said in his new deep voice. And, with a few powerful flaps, he soared into the air, grabbed the silver umbrella's handle and re-alighted next to the worried little group of friends.

'Look,' said Crab Far See. 'There's a little bottle tied to the handle and a note addressed to Lizard.'

D. H. Globule cleared his throat and began reading the note in his most important voice. 'My dear Lizard,' he began.

My dear Lizard,

The Royal Ducks of Planet Pluto send greetings, and will never forget your heroic actions. We will look after your tail for ever and ever. It will live in the Palace with my Dad. Thanks for the Ba-na-na-na-na.

Signed for and on behalf of Prince Whistling Tree Duck of Pluto.

P.S. Sprinkle a little of the stuff in the bottle onto what's left of your tail and all will be well.

Love from the Prince.

Suddenly everyone's mood changed and they all began laughing and cheering.

Ratty pulled the cork with his strong white teeth.

'Keep still, Lizard,' said the Crab. Carefully holding the little bottle in his claws, he began to sprinkle a sparkling, silver powder on the stump of Lizard's tail.

At first nothing happened. Then Lizard began to itch all over. A strange blueish light covered his entire body. The light became brighter and brighter. Everyone had to close their eyes, the light was so bright. Some wild goats ran off, bleating in fright. Then all was suddenly normal again. One by one the friends opened their eyes.

In the soft light of sunset, they all stared at the most beautiful tail they had ever seen. The magic potion from Planet Pluto had worked. The Lizard had a bigger and more splendid tail than ever!

Well, you can imagine how loud was the cheering and the shouting and how joyous was the dancing! At last, Lizard quietened them all down. Breathlessly, they stood around him and his glistening tail.

'Thank you, thank you, everyone,' he cried. 'But before anything else happens to us, it is definitely time for home.'

With his fine new tail on high, the happy Lizard led his friends in a dancing,

prancing

jig

down the mountain path.

Everyone, that is, except the Bungle Bird.

He had found an old tree stump, on which he was sitting and thinking. For a long time, he sat silent and alone in the feather-soft twilight. Then he made his decision. He stretched his wings and rose into the warm night air.

The still jubilant friends were half way down the mountain, when the graceful figure of a bird swooped and looped across the smiling face of old man moon.

'Quiet, everybody, listen! It's the Bungle and he's flying and actually singing,' whispered Lizard. And the Bungle Bird sang as he flew across the moon.

'Since I was small,
I've tried to fly,
Like other birds up to the sky,
Now have you heard,
I'M A BIRD
AND I CAN FLY!'

46

'Dear Bungle,' said Lizard softly, 'Gallons of luck, my good old friend.'
And, high above, the Bungle Bird and Old Man Moon flew on together
all through the gentle Caribbean night.

First published 1998 by
MACMILLAN EDUCATION LTD
London and Basingstoke
Companies and representatives throughout the world

ISBN 0–333–71022–3

10	9	8	7	6	5	4	3	2	1
07	06	05	04	03	02	01	00	99	98

This book is printed on paper suitable for recycling and
made from fully managed and sustained forest sources.

Printed in Hong Kong

Typset by EXPO Holdings, Malaysia

A catalogue record for this book is available from the
British Library.